D0961542

Ratty Tattletale

THE INFAMOUS RATSOS

Ratty Tattletale

Kara LaReau

illustrated by Matt Myers

CANDLEWICK PRESS

Text copyright © 2021 by Kara LaReau
Illustrations copyright © 2021 by Matt Myers

First edition 2021

Library of Congress Catalog Card Number pending
ISBN 978-1-5362-0746-0

20 21 22 23 24 25 LBM 10 9 8 7 6 5 4 3 2 1

Printed in Melrose Park, IL, USA

This book was typeset in Scala.
The illustrations were done in ink and watercolor dye on paper.

Candlewick Press
99 Dover Street
Somerville, Massachusetts 02144

www.candlewick.com

For those who do what's right,
even if it's not cool or easy
KL

For my mom, who taught me that
kindness takes courage
MM

TINY TOSS

It's Monday morning at Peter Rabbit
Elementary School, and not everyone is
happy about it in the third-grade line.

"I hate Mondays," says Ralphie.

"Same," says Millicent, yawning.

"Really? I love them," says Velma.

"Me, too!" says Tiny.

"You do?" asks Ralphie.

"Studies show that you do your best work on Mondays," Velma informs him. "It's also least likely to rain. And if you switch around the letters in *Monday*, it spells *dynamo*."

"Dynamo? I like the sound of that," says Millicent.

"I like how Mondays are like a fresh start," Tiny says. "Anything can happen!"

Just then, Kurt Musky sneaks behind Tiny and picks him up.

"Hey, who wants to play Tiny Toss?" yells Kurt.

"Me! Me!" says Sid Chitterer, laughing.

"Cut it out, guys!" yells Tiny. "I've told you before—I don't like being picked up, and I *definitely* don't like being tossed!"

As usual, Kurt and Sid don't listen.

"Aw, he's so *cute* when he's angry," says Sid.

"We're just kidding around. Stop being so uptight, Crawley," says Kurt.

"I'll stop being uptight when you put me *down*," says Tiny.

"Should we do something?" asks Velma.

"Maybe I should tell a teacher," says Millicent.

"Don't tell a teacher!" yells Tiny. "That'll make it worse!"

"How could it get any worse?" asks Ralphie.

"It can. Believe me," says Velma. "Last week Kurt and Sid brought gum to school, and after I told on them, I ended up with gum on my chair at lunch."

"Talk about a sticky situation," says Millicent.

"Come on, bro—toss him here!"
Sid shouts to Kurt, running down the
hall.

"No!" cries Tiny.

Finally, Ralphie steps in.

"If you guys don't put him down, you're going to be in TROUBLE," he says loudly.

"What's going on here?" asks Miss Beavers, the third-grade teacher.

"Nothing, ma'am," says Kurt. "We're just kidding around."

"Sid, Kurt, you know our school rule about respecting other people's personal space. Put Tiny down and follow me to the principal's office," Miss Beavers says.

"Thanks for ratting us out, Ratso," Sid whispers as Miss Beavers walks ahead.

"Now *you're* gonna be in trouble," says Kurt, cracking his knuckles.

"Ralphie, you're my hero," says Tiny. "You really saved my tail."

"Well, now I have to watch *my* tail," says Ralphie.

"Don't worry," says Millicent. "We'll all look out for you."

"Just look out for gum before you sit down anywhere," warns Velma.

"Now I *really* hate Mondays," Ralphie says.

2

SPLAT!

At least I made it to lunch," says Ralphie. "And they're serving my favorite—hot dogs."

When Sid and Kurt walk by, they flip Ralphie's lunch tray.

SPLAT!

"Whoops," says Sid, grinning.

"Try not to be so *clumsy*, Ratso," says Kurt.

"Ralphie, you'd better clean that up," says Principal Otteriguez. "We take responsibility for our messes at school."

By the time Ralphie finishes cleaning and gets to his table, all his friends have finished their lunches.

"What took you so long?" Louie asks. "And where's your lunch?"

"I . . . had some stuff to do. And . . .
I kinda lost my appetite," says Ralphie.

"Bummer," says Chad. "I was
gonna ask you if I could have your
pudding."

"We were just about to tell Louie about what happened this morning," says Tiny.

"You know," says Velma. "With the—"

"With the *Monday trivia*," Ralphie says, turning to his brother. "Did you know that it's least likely to rain on Mondays? And that if you switch around the letters in *Monday*, it spells *dynamo?*"

"Fascinating," says Louie. "I had no idea you were so into trivia."

"Time to line up, fifth-graders!" Mr. Ferretti announces.

"See you later, *dynamo*," Louie says, giving his brother a nudge.

"Why didn't you want us to tell your brother about what happened with Kurt and Sid?" Tiny asks after Louie and Chad and Fluffy leave.

"Because then he'd want to fix it. And I want to handle it myself," says Ralphie.

"Is that mustard on your shirt?" says Millicent. "And pudding?"

"Maybe," says Ralphie.

"It looks like Kurt and Sid have been handling *you*," says Millicent.

3

FRIENDLY COMPETITION

That afternoon on the playground, Ralphie breathes a sigh of relief.

"At least I made it to recess all in one piece," he says. "Well, except for my lunch. And my shirt."

"Miss Beavers brought out all the playground equipment," says Millicent. "We can play bombardment!"

"Can't we just play dodgeball?" asks Tiny.

"Bombardment is more fun," says Ralphie. "It's basically dodgeball, but everyone has a chance to get a ball and throw it at the opposing team."

"One ball is more than enough for me," says Tiny.

"Don't worry," says Velma. "You're the smallest, so you're the hardest target to hit."

"I like the way you think," says Tiny.

Just as Ralphie and his classmates are drawing up teams, one of the fifth-grade classes comes out for recess. Including Kurt and Sid.

"Oh, no," says Ralphie. "Why couldn't we be sharing recess with Louie's fifth-grade class?"

"Check it out," Sid says to Kurt. "The little third-graders are getting ready to play bombardment, our favorite game."

"Nothing we like more than a little friendly competition," Kurt says, cracking his knuckles. He and Sid join the team opposite Ralphie's.

"As long as you keep it *friendly*," says Millicent.

"Get ready, kids," says Miss Beavers. "Get set . . ."

TWEET!

When she blows her whistle, everyone races to grab one of the balls. Ralphie manages to get one, and throws it at Millicent.

"Gotcha! You're out!" he says.

"Oh, well. Good one, Ralphie," says Millicent. She gives him a high-five, then joins Velma and the other tagged-out kids on the sidelines.

"Don't get cocky, Ratso," says Sid. He and Kurt both have balls, and they're aiming them right at Ralphie.

"You're not supposed to aim for someone's head," says Ralphie.

"We don't play by third-grade *baby* rules," says Sid.

"Get ready to get bombarded," says Kurt.

Sid and Kurt throw the balls as hard as they can.

"Look out, Ralphie!" Velma cries from the sidelines.

But before Ralphie knows what he's doing, he catches one—then the other.

"Whoa," says Millicent.

"Ha!" says Ralphie. "You're both out!"

TWEET!

Miss Beavers blows her whistle.

"You're out, too, Ralphie," she says. "You know the rules—you're not supposed to hold more than one ball at a time."

"Aw, *man*," says Ralphie.

"Tiny, that means you won!" Velma says.

"Hooray!" cries Tiny. "This must be my lucky day!"

"And my *unlucky* day," mutters Ralphie, as Sid and Kurt give him the stink eye.

4

RATTY TATTLETALE

On the way home, let's make sure to stop by Mrs. Porcupini's," Louie says after school. "She always has treats for us."

"Sure," says Ralphie. "I just need to get my backpack. I could have sworn I hung it right here in my cubby."

Ralphie looks all around the cubbies. He looks on the floor. He looks around his classroom. No backpack.

And then he sees it. In the trash can.

"How did it get in there?" Louie asks.

"Beats me," says Ralphie, but he knows exactly how it got there. Because there's a note pinned to the front, which he hides from Louie. It says:

PREPARE TO GET TRASHED

"Um . . . how about we go a different way home from school today? Maybe we can find a new shortcut," Ralphie suggests.

"Don't be silly," says Louie, walking ahead. "Don't you want some of Mrs. Porcupini's treats?"

"What I really want is to not get *trashed*," Ralphie mutters.

"Why do you keep looking over your shoulder?" Louie asks as they walk home.

"I was . . . just thinking about finding that shortcut," says Ralphie.

"OK, let's go a different way after Mrs. Porcupini's," says Louie. "She's right around the corner."

The Ratso brothers used to think Mrs. Porcupini was mean, but it turns out she's really nice, *and* she's an excellent baker.

"Want to try my chocolate-chip pretzel cookies?" she asks. "They're fresh from the oven!"

"Don't mind if I do," says Louie. "*Yum.*"

But Ralphie can't enjoy his. He keeps looking over his shoulder.

"I can't believe you're not eating yours," says Louie. "You didn't have any lunch, so you must be starving."

"Maybe I'm coming down with something," Ralphie says.

"Now that you mention it, you do look a little sweaty," says Louie.

"How are the cookies, boys?" Mrs. Porcupini asks.

"I think they're tasty—but I'll need another one to be sure," says Louie.

"I'll get you some nice cold milk to go with them," Mrs. Porcupini says, disappearing inside.

Ralphie is finally about to take a bite of his when Sid and Kurt round the corner.

"You can have mine," Ralphie says to Louie. "I think I've lost my appetite again."

Kurt cracks his knuckles. "Well, well, well," he says. "If it isn't our old pal Ratty Tattletale."

"I didn't tattle on you," Ralphie insists.

"What's this about?" says Louie.

"Nothing," Ralphie says.

"It's not nothing that you got us sent to the principal's office this morning," Sid says.

"You got yourself sent there, for picking on Tiny," Ralphie says. "I just told you to stop."

"You just need to mind your own business, Ratso," says Kurt.

"Leave him *alone*," says Louie.

"Aw, now you got your big brother sticking up for you?" Sid says. "How sweet."

"Did someone say sweets?" says Mrs. Porcupini, appearing with glasses of milk. "I have more cookies if you boys want some."

"No thanks. We've got planning to do," Kurt says, cracking his knuckles again.

"Yeah, you're never gonna know what hit you, Ratso," Sid says as they walk off. "See you around."

"Was that what the other kids were trying to tell me at lunch today,

when you stopped them?" Louie asks Ralphie. "Why didn't you want me to know that Kurt and Sid are picking on you? I'm the big brother—I'm supposed to protect you."

"Because I don't need protecting. I can handle this myself," Ralphie insists.

"Well, Kurt and Sid shouldn't be threatening you," Louie says. "Maybe you should tell a teacher, or Principal Otteriguez. Or Dad."

"I don't want to rat out Kurt and Sid. That's not cool," Ralphie says.

"You know what else isn't cool?" Louie says. "Being bullied."

"Believe me, I *know*," says Ralphie.

5

DON'T TELL

That night, **Ralphie** barely manages to eat dinner.

"What's wrong?" Big Lou asks. "You usually love my mac and cheese with bacon and peas."

Ralphie opens his mouth. He really, really wants to tell his dad what's wrong. But he just can't.

"I think I'm coming down with something," he says.

"Actually, he's—" Louie begins.

Ralphie kicks his brother under the table. He gives Louie a look. Louie knows that it means "Don't tell."

Louie sighs. "Actually, he hasn't eaten all day," he says.

Big Lou feels Ralphie's forehead.

"You don't feel hot," says Big Lou. "But maybe we should keep you home from school tomorrow, just to be safe."

"But, Dad, you have that new forklift job starting tomorrow at the Big City Warehouse," Louie says.

"Some things are more important than a paycheck," Big Lou says. He turns to Ralphie. "Now, let's get you into your pajamas and into bed."

Louie kicks Ralphie under the table and gives him a look. Ralphie knows what it means. It's bad enough not telling their dad the whole truth; it's even worse to make him miss work because of it.

"I . . . think I'll be OK to go to school tomorrow," Ralphie says. "I don't feel that bad."

"Let's play it by ear, kiddo. You don't need to tough it out," Big Lou says.

But that's exactly what Ralphie decides to do.

– 6 –
PING!

Wow," Chad says when he sees Ralphie at lunch the next day. "You look rough."

"I didn't sleep last night," Ralphie says.

"Why not?" asks Fluffy.

"Kurt and Sid have been picking on him," Louie explains.

"And I can't stop worrying about what they're going to do next," Ralphie says.

"I feel like this is my fault," Tiny says. "If you didn't step in to defend me, Sid and Kurt wouldn't be after *you*."

"Yeah, but then they'd still be after you," Velma reminds him.

"Good point," says Tiny.

"Why don't I just go say something to Kurt and Sid now?" says Chad.

"You're the biggest kid in the fifth grade. You can just *look* at them and they'll leave Ralphie alone," Tiny says.

"Thanks, but I don't need anyone else fighting my battles," says Ralphie.

"Do you need someone eating your brownie?" asks Chad.

Ping!

"Ouch," says Ralphie.

"What is it?" says Louie.

Ping!

"Ouch!" says Ralphie. He rubs the back of his head. "Something just hit me."

At the next table, Sid and Kurt are holding what look like straws.

"Peashooters?" says Millicent. "Ugh, those two."

"Peashooters are *definitely* against the rules," says Velma.

Ping!

"Take that, *pea brain*!" says Sid.

"Cut it OUT!" yells Ralphie.

"No yelling in the cafeteria," says Principal Otteriguez. "You know the rules, Ralphie."

"Sorry, sir," says Ralphie.

"Tell Principal Otteriguez about the peashooters," Louie says. "Sid and Kurt shouldn't have them in school."

"They could really hurt someone," says Fluffy.

"I'm not a Ratty Tattletale," Ralphie says.

Ping!

"OUCH!" he cries. "That one really hurt!"

"I told you to stop yelling, Ralphie," Principal Otteriguez says. "I'll see you in my office after lunch."

"Life just keeps getting better and better," Ralphie says.

"I'll see you after school," says Louie.

"Righto," says Ralphie. "I need to make a stop on the way home. It's time I stuck up for myself."

- 7 -

UH-OH

I don't think this is a good plan," Louie says, slurping his Big Claw soda on their way home from Clawmart.

"I think it's my only plan," says Ralphie. "Don't they say you need to fight fire with fire?"

"I don't know who 'they' are, but I don't think they were talking about peashooters," Louie says. "I can't believe you spent all your money on that thing."

"This *thing* is going to help me defend myself," says Ralphie. He unwraps the package and looks at the instructions. "Wait a minute. 'Peas sold separately'? What a rip-off!"

"Maybe you can use something else," says Louie. "How about my straw wrapper?"

Ralphie tries it. *Pfft*. The balled-up wrapper floats to the ground.

"It's too light. I need something more like a pea, I guess," he says.

"How about a little pebble?" says Louie.

The Ratso brothers look all over the sidewalk.

"Ah, here's a good one," says Ralphie. He sticks the pebble in one end of his peashooter, then he blows in the other. "It's not moving."

"Maybe the pebble is too big," says

Louie. "What do the instructions say?"

Ralphie looks at them. "They say

'Only for use with peas.' Aw, now it's

broken? I didn't even get to use it!"

"I bet it's not broken, just stuck,"

says Louie. "Here, give it to me."

Louie puts the peashooter in his mouth. He takes a deep breath, then blows as hard as he can.

PING!

The pebble ricochets off a trash can . . .

and goes through Mrs. Porcupini's big front window with a

SMASH!

"Uh-oh," says Louie. "I guess I overdid it."

"You *guess*?" says Ralphie.

"My window!" Mrs. Porcupini cries. "My beautiful window!"

"It was an accident!" says Louie.

"How will I ever afford to replace it?" Mrs. Porcupini says.

"We're so sorry!" says Ralphie.

"*We're* so sorry?" Louie says, giving his brother a nudge.

"You're right. *You* should be the one apologizing, since technically, you did it," Ralphie reminds him.

"But *you* bought the peashooter in the first place," Louie says. "I was just helping."

"Well, you can really help now—by spending *your* money on a new window," Ralphie says.

"Too late," Louie says. "I already blew it all on the Big Claw."

8

DOING WHAT'S RIGHT

I'm not mad. I'm *disappointed*," says Big Lou, when the Ratso brothers tell him what happened.

"I hate when you're disappointed," says Louie.

"I almost wish you were mad," says Ralphie.

"Getting angry won't solve this. Just like getting a *peashooter* won't solve your problem with Sid and Kurt," says Big Lou. "What were you *thinking*, Ralphie?"

"I guess I wasn't," Ralphie says. "I just wanted them to stop picking on me."

"Violence is never the answer," says Big Lou. "Everywhere I go, people always try to pick fights with me, because I look tough. But I'm too smart to take the bait."

"What do you do instead?" asks Louie.

"Sometimes I reason with them. Sometimes I make a joke. And sometimes I just walk away," Big Lou explains.

"None of those things was going to stop Kurt and Sid from shooting peas at me," Ralphie says.

"If someone is picking on you, you can try to solve it yourself. But if they won't listen, or if they're hurting you or someone else, you always tell a grown-up you trust," Big Lou says.

"Like Miss Beavers, or Principal Otteriguez," Louie says to Ralphie.

"Or *me*," says Big Lou. "I had a feeling there was something going on with you last night. We could have figured it out together before it got this far."

"But isn't being a tattletale uncool?" Ralphie asks.

"Doing what's right is more important than what's cool," says Big Lou. "We're all going to go to school tomorrow to tell Principal Otteriguez about Sid and Kurt and those peashooters. You could have lost an eye, or worse!"

"You're right, Dad," says Ralphie.

"And I don't care if Clawmart says it's a toy—a peashooter is a *weapon*. It's not something you play around with, especially on the street," Big Lou says.

"I think we've both learned a lesson," says Louie.

"Well, just to be sure, you two are going to have to pay for a new window for Mrs. Porcupini," Big Lou says.

"How are we going to do that? We don't have any money!" Louie says.

"You'll figure it out," says Big Lou. "Aren't you the one who always has a plan?"

"He's right, big brother," says Ralphie. "Start thinking."

9

A VERY GENEROUS DONATION

Toys for sale!" Louie yells.

"Mostly new and partly used toys for sale!" yells Ralphie.

"A sidewalk sale?" says Mrs. McMoley. "How quaint."

"Want to buy something?" asks Ralphie. "I have a whole set of Super Critter figures here, and most of them still have their arms and legs."

"No, thank you. I'm just browsing," she says.

"If you change your mind, we'll be here all day!" Louie calls after her.

"All day," says Ralphie, sighing. "I can't believe we're stuck out here all Saturday, selling these junky toys."

"Like you had a better idea?" Louie says.

"Hey, guys," says Tiny.

"Boy, are we glad to see you," says Ralphie. "Want to buy some toys?"

"We're just here for moral support," says Velma.

"Thanks, everyone," says Louie.

"I should have given those two a piece of my mind, even when you told me not to," says Chad.

"Nah. I should have handled it myself, the right way," says Ralphie.

"Look, it's Kurt and Sid!" says Millicent.

"And their parents," says Fluffy.

"What happened to you guys?" asks Tiny.

"We got bored using our peashooters on other people," says Kurt.

"So we started shooting at each other," says Sid. "The doctor says our eyes should be good as new in a week. Which works out, since that's how long Principal Otteriguez suspended us."

"I'm glad those two finally learned their lesson," Millicent whispers to Velma.

"Too bad they had to learn it the hard way," Velma replies, shaking her head.

"Is there something you want to say to your friends, Sidney?" says Mrs. Chitterer.

"Go on, son," Mr. Chitterer says, giving Sid a nudge.

Sid takes a deep breath. "I'm—I'm sorry for what I did," he says. "Bullying is wrong."

"Your turn, Kurtis," says Mrs. Musky.

"I'm . . . sorry, too," says Kurt. "For the bullying. And the peashooting."

"And how about the *Tiny Tossing*?" adds Tiny.

"OK, that, too," says Kurt.

"We were just kidding around," says Sid.

"It didn't feel like kidding around to me," says Tiny.

"We saw the signs at school for your sidewalk sale," says Mrs. Musky. "Sidney and Kurtis would like to make a very generous donation."

"Here," says Kurt.

"Take mine, too," says Sid.

"Your peashooters?" says Louie, looking through the pile. "And your slingshots, *and* your BB guns?"

"Now they're all yours," says Mrs. Chitterer. "Or whoever wants to buy them."

"I'll buy them," says Big Lou. "And your peashooter, too, Ralphie."

"Dad?" says Ralphie.

10

A FAIR DEAL

Yep," says Big Lou. "I'll buy all of them. I'm going to donate them to the Big City Scouts. If you want to use them there, you'll have to get proper instruction, so you can learn the right way to handle them—*with supervision.*"

"And then we can earn our Bull's-eye badges!" Sid says, elbowing Kurt.

Big Lou hands Louie and Ralphie some money. "You can use this to buy Mrs. Porcupini a new window."

"Thank you, Dad," says Louie.

"Thank you, thank you, thank you," says Ralphie.

"Not so fast," says Big Lou. "In exchange, I want you to wash that new window every Saturday for three months."

"Three months?" says Ralphie.

Louie gives his brother a look. "It's a fair deal," he says.

"Is someone making some deals?" asks Mrs. Porcupini. "I heard about the sidewalk sale, and I thought you might need some refreshments."

"We're sorry again about your window, ma'am," Ralphie says.

"We both are," adds Louie.

"Apology accepted, boys," says Mrs. Porcupini. "Having it boarded up for a little while is actually a good thing—since I'm not staring out of it all the time, I'm more focused on my baking."

"Ooh, homemade cookies and lemonade," says Chad. "This is the best sidewalk sale I've ever been to!"

"This is the *only* sidewalk sale we've ever been to," Velma reminds him.

"It looks like we can already pay for that window for you, Mrs. Porcupini," Louie says.

"I call that a smashing success!" says Ralphie.

Kara LaReau is the author of the previous books in the Infamous Ratsos series, illustrated by Matt Myers, as well as the middle-grade series the ZomBert Chronicles, illustrated by Ryan Andrews. She is also the author of several picture books, including *Baby Clown*, illustrated by Matthew Cordell. About this book, she says, "Like Louie and Ralphie and their friends, I don't always make the right choices, but I try to learn from my mistakes and do better." Kara LaReau lives in Providence, Rhode Island.

Matt Myers is the illustrator of the previous titles in the Infamous Ratsos series by Kara LaReau. He is also the author-illustrator of *Hum and Swish* and has illustrated numerous other picture books, including *Pirate's Perfect Pet* by Beth Ferry. About this book, he says, "Standing up *to* a bully doesn't usually accomplish much. But standing up *for* someone who is being bullied changes the world." Matt Myers lives in Charlotte, North Carolina.

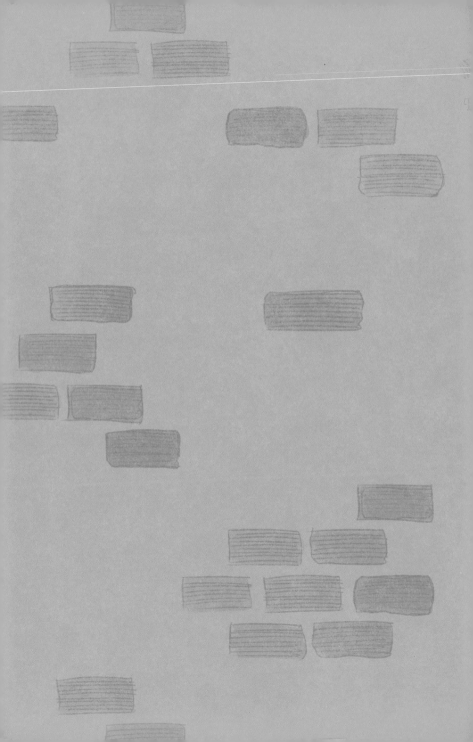